D1532011

YOU CHEAT!

By Jamie Gilson
Illustrated by Maxie Chambliss

Bradbury Press • New York
Maxwell Macmillan Canada • Toronto
Maxwell Macmillan International
New York • Oxford • Singapore • Sydney

Comsewogue Public Library
170 Terryville Road
Port Jefferson Station NY 11776

Text copyright © 1992 by Jamie Gilson
Illustrations copyright © 1992 by Maxie Chambliss

All rights reserved. No part of this book may be reproduced or transmitted
in any form or by any means, electronic or mechanical, including photo-
copying, recording, or by any information storage and retrieval system,
without permission in writing from the Publisher.

Bradbury Press
Macmillan Publishing Company
866 Third Avenue
New York, NY 10022

Maxwell Macmillan Canada, Inc.
1200 Eglinton Avenue East
Suite 200
Don Mills, Ontario M3C 3N1

Macmillan Publishing Company is part of the Maxwell Communication
Group of Companies.

First American edition
Printed and bound in Hong Kong
by South China Printing Company (1988) Ltd.

10 9 8 7 6 5 4 3 2 1

The text of this book is set in Korinna.
The illustrations are rendered in pen-and-ink and watercolor.

Library of Congress Cataloging-in-Publication Data

Gilson, Jamie.
You cheat! / by Jamie Gilson; illustrated by Maxie Chambliss.—
1st American ed.
p.   cm.
Summary: Nathan bribes his older brother to go fishing, and then
wishes he hadn't.
ISBN 0-02-735993-X
[1. Fishing—Fiction. 2. Brothers—Fiction.] 1. Chambliss,
Maxie, ill. II. Title.
PZ7.G4385 Yo   1992
[E]—dc20   91-13886

For Rick Wiegel,
who did it

—J.G.

For Morgan,
who helped

—M.C.

CONTENTS

GO

"*I'll play Go Fish one time,*" *Hank* said. He curled up in the wicker chair and flicked on his hand-held video game. "But that's all. You get it ready. I'm busy." He could hear raindrops *ping* on the porch roof. He began to push buttons. Then all he could hear was *beep beep beep splat.*

His brother, Nathan, tore open the Go
Fish box. It was brand-new. Nathan
shook the jumbo cards from the box and
placed them carefully on the porch rug,
fish-side down. Then, kneeling forward,
he swirled them around and around.

"Mix them good," Hank called, without
looking up from his game. Hank was
eight, and he liked giving orders to

Nathan. Nathan was six. "And no fair peeking," Hank told him. "You always cheat."

"Liar, liar, pants on fire," Nathan said. He whirled the cards faster. One flipped over. The gray fish on it had sharp teeth, a sailor hat cocked to the side, and a little heart tattooed on its fin.

3

"Cheater, cheater, toe-jam eater!"
Hank yelled. "I saw that. You peeked."

"Did not," Nathan said, turning the
card back over.

"Did, too," Hank called. But he didn't
really care. He was smashing snakes just
by pushing a button. *Splat.*

"Ready, get set, go fish," Nathan called.

Splat. Beep. Beep. Beep. Beep. Splat. The only part of Hank set to go was his thumb.

"All you do is play that dumb game. You've got to play with me while we're here," Nathan told him. "Mom said. If you don't, I'll tell."

Hank and Nathan were staying for two weeks with Aunt Paula. Aunt Paula lived in a cabin on a lake in the country. In the city they lived eight floors up.

Hank sighed. "Bor-ing." But he zapped off his game and sank to the floor. He took six cards, looked at them, and grinned.

"You know how to play this?" he asked.
"You've got to get four all alike. Like this."
He put four yellow fish cards faceup on
the rug. "I win."

Nathan shook his head. "No, you don't. You cheat! The guy with the most sets wins. I played this in kindergarten."

"It's a baby game," Hank said, and he looked at his cards again. "Okay. Still my turn. Got any red ones?" he asked.

Nathan bit his lip. "You saw," he said. "I bet you saw." Then, because there was nothing else to do, he handed over his three red fish.

Hank took them and added a red card from his own hand. "That makes four." He grinned at Nathan. "Give up?" he asked.

STOP

Hank won the first game. He also won the second. After he won the third he said, "Time to stop. I'm champion of all fish." He took a yellow apple from a bowl on the porch table and began to shine it on his T-shirt.

Nathan took an apple, too, and bit into it.

"You got to watch out with apples,"
Hank told him as he watched Nathan
swallow. "I always check before I chew.
Worms live inside apples. If you're not
careful, you snap them in half."

Nathan looked where he had bitten.
He did not see a worm hole.

"Sometimes," Hank went on, "they slide down so easy you don't even know you got one. Sometimes you swallow them hole and all."

Nathan took another bite. To show how brave he was he didn't even look first.

"I bet I know more about worms than you do," he told Hank. "When Aunt Paula and I went fishing I stuck worms on a hook. They were fat and juicy. I did it yesterday, and I did it the day before. You were way too scared to come."

"I was way too busy," Hank said, picking up his video game.

"I caught three fish yesterday," Nathan told him.

Hank rolled his eyes. "I know that. Who wants to catch fish, anyway?"

"I ate them fried for supper," Nathan said. "I got to use their tails for handles. My fish were delicious."

"My hot dog was better," Hank told him. "Hot dogs are better than anything. And they don't have tails."

Nathan turned all forty cards faceup and made them swim in circles. Then suddenly he looked outside. "You know what?" he said. "It's stopped raining. Let's go fish."

"I said I'd play Go Fish one time, and I played three," Hank told him. He bent

over the video game in his hand, pushing
buttons till it went wild with beeps of vic-
tory. Then he smiled and said, "Thank
you, thank you," bowing to Nathan, to the
empty wicker chair, and even to Horse-
shoe Lake, outside the big screened
porch.

"I don't want to go fish for cards," Nathan said. "I want to go fish for fish. I bet I won't lose doing that." He pushed the cards aside and stood up. "I'll ask Aunt Paula."

As Nathan hurried away, Hank frowned and took a giant bite of his shiny apple. He waited, chewing, hoping for a "no."

"Al*right*!" Nathan called from inside. "We can. We can go fish!"

The sun began to shine. A warm breeze blew in from the lake.

Hank frowned again. He started to take another bite of apple. But before he did, he looked. And then he looked again, closer.

Right in the middle of the white part, between the marks he'd made with his two front teeth, there it was. It was a hole where half a worm had once lived.

CAUTION

"*They smell okay,*" *Aunt Paula said.*
"I got these guys two days ago at Kmart
for two forty-five." She held out a carton
that looked as though it should hold cot-
tage cheese. On the lid it said in big green
letters, 24 CANADIAN NIGHT CRAWLERS.
"What d'you think?" She pried open the
lid and showed Hank and Nathan.

The carton was filled with damp black dirt. Two worms as fat as Hank's little finger squirmed on top. He felt sick, remembering the hole in the apple.

"You sure you can do this without me?" Aunt Paula went on. "I'd love to help, but I've stacks of work to do."

"We're okay," Nathan told her. "We'll just fish off the pier like you and I did yesterday."

"I'll stay inside like I did yesterday," Hank said. "There are mosquitoes outside. And flies. And bees."

"And good fresh air and trees," Aunt Paula told him.

"And bluegill fish," Nathan added.

"Besides," Aunt Paula went on, "your mother sent you here to soak up nature, and not, I think, to become video game master of the universe." She handed Nathan the carton of worms. "I'll spread my work out on the porch table and watch from here. Use caution, though. Don't prick your fingers with the hooks. And, of course, don't fall in the water."

"Sounds dangerous," Hank said. "I think I'll wait."

"Nonsense," Aunt Paula told him. "There's danger everywhere. At home you have to look out every time you cross a street. You just have to be careful."

The screen door slammed. Nathan was already outside. He was heading to the shed to get the poles.

Fish are sharp and slippery, Hank thought. Big ones bite people's legs off. "Are there sharks?" he asked.

Aunt Paula smiled. "There are *no* sharks in my lake," she told him. "The bluegills you're likely to catch are the size of your hand."

Hank looked at his hand. With his fingers closed, it looked little — for a fish. With his fingers spread, it looked big. Still, a fish that size couldn't take off your leg. It might eat half a toe.

"You'll be fine," Aunt Paula said. "If you drop your video game in the water, though, it will never beep again."

Hank stared out at the lake. It looked dark and deep.

"Throw back the littlest ones," Aunt Paula went on. "I'll cook what you catch. I'll even clean it for you."

Clean it. Hank knew what that meant. It meant chopping off the fish's head, scraping off its scales, and pulling out its ooshy insides.

Fishing is disgusting, Hank said to himself. I won't do it. I'll watch Nathan. One time. But that's all. He left his video game on the chair, opened the door, and started down the steps.

The trees scattered leftover rain on him as he walked as slowly as possible to the pier.

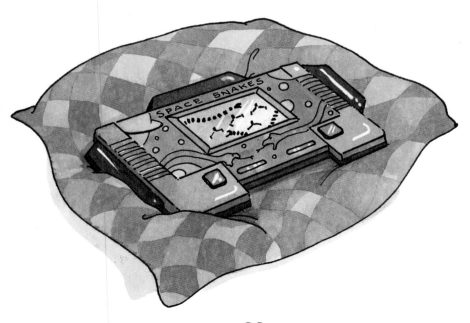

PLOP

Nathan was already at the end of the pier. He set down a bucket and two bamboo poles. Carefully, he rolled a rubber band off the end of his pole. That let the line and the hook swing free.

"Shhhhh," he told Hank, pressing his finger on his lips. "Don't scare the fish. They'll run away."

Hank picked up a stone, tossed it into the water, and looked out for running fish. A tree had fallen into the lake and nobody had pulled it out. This was not water to swim in. There were things in it, like branches and lily pads, and weeds. And beneath them, things with open mouths were hiding.

Hank stomped as hard as he could on the wooden planks of the pier.

"Shhhhh," Nathan said again.

Nathan flipped the lid off the 24 Canadian Night Crawlers carton. The dirt inside was moving.

Nathan didn't care. He dug in, pulled out a long fat worm, and put it in the palm of his hand.

"You know how to tell which end is which?" he whispered to Hank.

Hank looked. He couldn't tell.

The worm crept toward Nathan's fingers. "It walks headfirst. That's how." He wagged the worm in front of Hank's nose, and then put it on the pier.

"Bluegills are so little you've got to cut their food for them," he explained. He took a small pair of scissors from the bucket. Then, without even saying

"yuck," he zipped off a piece of worm the size of a jelly bean.

Hank listened. The worm did not scream. The big piece and the little piece both wiggled. "I don't like this," Hank said. "I don't like this at all."

"You are a scaredy-cat," Nathan told him.

"Am not," Hank said, but he was afraid maybe it was true. "I just *like* worms. Really. Maybe it's got a name."

"See this?" Nathan asked him. He held up a small plastic ball that was stuck to his fishing line. "This is a bobber. Aunt Paula says it holds the worm up. It keeps it off the bottom of the lake." He flicked his line out so the hook fell in the shade of the fallen tree.

From the porch Aunt Paula called,
"How you guys doing?"

Nathan waved back. Hank crossed his
arms.

"There's a big one under there,"
Nathan said quietly. "It's getting ready to
bite. It's getting ready to bite...right...
now!"

Nothing happened.

Nothing kept happening. For three minutes nothing happened. For five minutes. Then a small frog hopped onto the pier.

"That's a toad," Nathan told Hank. "You better not touch it, or you'll get warts."

"Will not."

"Will, too."

"It's not a toad," Hank said. He knew from second grade what it was. "It's a frog. Frogs are smooth. Toads are bumpy."

"I know what it really is," Nathan said.

"What?"

"A prince. Soon as a princess kisses it, it'll turn into one."

"That's bogus," Hank said.

"It was in a story in a book."

"A bogus book."

"I bet," Nathan said, "she wouldn't *want* to kiss it. I bet it's yucky."

"Yeah," Hank said, "and slimy like a fish."

Before a princess had time to walk by, the frog jumped into the high weeds.

The water was still.

"This is bor-ing," Hank said. He wanted to push a button to make something happen.

"Oh, I forgot," Nathan told him. And holding his fishing pole in one hand, he dug in the dirt with the other. He pulled out a new worm, even bigger and fatter than the last. "This is yours."

Hank didn't reach for the worm, so Nathan put it on his brother's arm. The worm began to crawl.

"Go fish," Nathan said.

NO!

The worm squirmed. Hank didn't like it. He didn't want to pet it. He didn't want to give it a name. It was not his friend. He wanted it out of there.

"Gross," he said, and shook the worm onto the pier. He didn't pick it up. It slipped between the boards and dropped into the water.

"No fair. That's free food," Nathan told him. "Now they won't take mine. No fair."

"I'm going back to the cabin to get my game," Hank said.

"Scaredy-cat, scaredy-cat. Scared of where the fish are at."

"Am not," Hank said. But he didn't leave.

Nathan took his sneakers off and dangled his toes in the lake.

"Look at that," he whispered. Then he started to giggle. "That fish just nibbled my toe."

Hank looked. He saw a fish dart away. "Is it bleeding?" he asked.

Nathan held up his toe. "He only licked it."

The bobber sat still in the water. No fish pulled it under.

"This is no fun," Hank said. He wished he was sitting in the soft chair with his game.

"That's because you're not fishing. I'll cut the worm and stick it on the hook for you," Nathan said. "Then will you do it?"

"No way," Hank told him.

"I'll cut the worm, stick it on the hook, *and* throw it in," Nathan said. "Then will you?"

"No way."

"I'll give you five cents. I've got five cents in my pocket," Nathan said. He stood up, took the nickel out, and showed it.

"That won't buy anything," Hank said.

"In the cabin I've got the five dollars Mom gave me. If you fish, I'll give you five dollars."

"If I took it, you'd cry."

"I don't need it," Nathan told him. "You do. You always want to buy stuff. Five dollars if you fish."

Hank didn't say no.

"For five dollars you've got to squish the worm on the hook. *And* throw it in the lake."

"No," Hank said. "I won't. I won't kill it. That's gross."

"You step on spiders," Nathan told him. He stood up and lifted his line out of the water. The worm slice was still there. He flipped it back in again near some lily pads. "You swat flies."

"Worms," Hank said, "are different."

"My bobber," Nathan called. "Look! My bobber is bouncing. Look at that. Look! It's gone. I can feel it. I can feel it pulling. I've got one!"

Nathan lifted his pole high till you could see the end of the line.

And it was true. Nathan had caught a fish.

YES!

"Can I take the hook out?" Nathan yelled to Aunt Paula. "Can I do it myself?"

"Go for it," she called back.

Sliding the spiny fins back so they wouldn't scratch him, Nathan cupped the fish in his hand and eased the hook out of its mouth.

"Get me the stringer in the bucket," he told Hank. Hank didn't do it. He didn't like Nathan giving him orders.

"If my fish gets away, it's your fault," Nathan said.

Hank reached into the bucket and pulled out a long thick string with a sharp end like a needle.

Nathan took it from him and threaded the string through one of the fish's blue gills. The fish hung on the string like a single shiny bead on a huge necklace.

He looped one end of the string over a post and let the fish drop in the water.

"That's to keep it cool and fresh," Nathan explained.

Nathan sounded as if he thought he knew it all. Hank started toward the house. He'd had just about enough of Nathan.

"It's really fun," Nathan called to him. "You won't do it for five dollars?"

"Nope," Hank called over his shoulder.

"Ten?"

"You don't have ten."

That was true.

Nathan looked down at the fish flipping in the water.

"What if..." he tried. "What if..."

Hank was halfway back to the cabin.

"What if," Nathan yelled again, "every fish you catch I..."

Hank stopped to hear what Nathan would try next.

"What if every fish you catch, I...kiss on the mouth?"

"You what?" Hank backed up.

"I kiss on the mouth."

"You wouldn't do that. You wouldn't kiss a fish. I know you. You cheat."

"I do not. I bet I'd really kiss it."

"You're just saying that because you think I'm going to say no."

Nathan grinned.

"Wait a minute," Hank said. "You don't really believe the fish would turn into a princess?"

"Oh, no," Nathan said. "Not in a million years."

Hank was glad Nathan didn't believe stuff like that. He was never sure what Nathan believed. Nathan wasn't dumb, but he *was* little.

"It wouldn't do that," Nathan went on.

"It'd be your fish. *You'd* have to kiss it for that to happen. If you catch a fish, I'll kiss it. Cross my heart and hope to die. Stick my nose in cherry pie."

Hank walked onto the pier again. He looked down at the bluegill on the stringer. He thought about it — Nathan kissing that scaly, squirmy fish on its mouth. He held his teeth together hard. He held his breath, too, and he reached into the Kmart worm carton. Some things, he decided, are just too good to miss.

KISS KISS

Hank slid the rubber band off the pole to free the hook the way Nathan told him to. Then, wrinkling his nose, he cut the worm's tail off and stuck it on the hook the way Nathan told him to. Finally, he flung the hook into a shady spot, even though Nathan told him to.

And then he waited.

While Hank waited, Nathan caught a fish, another bluegill. He took it off his line and laced it on the stringer. "I'm a pro," he said.

Aunt Paula waved to them from the porch. "Looks like we'll have a banquet tonight," she called.

Hank felt a tug, an easy tug, on his pole. If this was a video creature, he thought, I could zap it away.

The bobber on his line bobbed and then it disappeared. The end of Hank's pole bent toward the water.

"I think," Hank said quietly, "I think your girlfriend is on the end of my line."

"You got a fish!" Nathan yelled, like he wasn't scared at all. "Or maybe you bagged an old boot."

"It's trying to get away," Hank said.

"Pull. Pull hard."

Hank pulled. The fish pulled, too.

Hank pulled harder. The fish was swimming in circles.

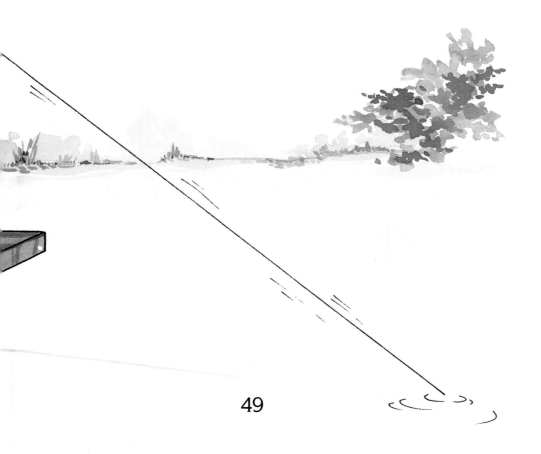

Hank tugged. Then he lifted his pole high. He had caught a real fish. All by himself he'd caught a fish. There it was waving on the end of his line. And it was some fish.

"That's not a bluegill," Nathan said.

"It's a fish," Hank told him. "You said you'd kiss any fish I caught."

"But it's gross," Nathan said. "That's the grossest fish I ever saw."

"It's mine." Hank leaned back with the pole and flipped the fish onto the pier. Nathan was right. The fish was ugly. Its face looked like it could star in Godzilla movies. It had feelers, long fat feelers.

"You've got to kiss it," Hank said, "on the mouth. You said cross your heart and hope to die."

Nathan had said it.

The fish flopped on the pier. Its feelers wagged. This one wouldn't turn into a princess, Nathan decided. This one would turn into a dragon. He thought about running. He thought hard about running.

Hank pulled up his line so the fish hung as high as Nathan's nose. It looked even uglier close up. "I bet you won't do it," he said.

"I bet I will." Nathan took a deep breath, aimed for a place between the feelers, and then, fast, pressed his mouth lightly on the fish's. It felt cool and wet. He stepped back quickly to see if it would change into a fire-snorting monster.

The fish flipped its tail, threw back its head, freed its mouth of the hook, and somersaulted *splat* into the lake again.

Nathan wiped his mouth on his sleeve.

"It's gone," Hank said. "My fish is gone. It was a lot bigger than yours. What did you do to it?"

"It didn't like me," Nathan told him.

They both stared where the fish had jumped. The water was as dark and quiet as a turned-off TV.

Hank shook his head. "That was fun," he said. "You never told me fishing was so much fun." He reached for another worm. "Maybe this time I'll catch a bigger one with even more feelers for you to kiss."

"It's too late," Nathan said, wiping his mouth again. "I'm done." He pulled his string of bluegills out of the water. "But I didn't cheat," he said.

Aunt Paula was walking down from the cabin, carrying a pitcher of lemonade and three blue cups. "Stopping already?" she asked. "I thought I saw someone catch a huge catfish."

"That was me," Hank told her. "But it got away."

"Slippery fellow," Aunt Paula said.

Nathan grabbed the cup with his fish-sticky hand and gulped down the lemonade. "Catfish?" he asked.

"Catfish," she said. "They're not so pretty, but they're good eating. You've got to be careful with them, though. They've got sharp fins that sting."

"It was a stinging monster. I caught a monster," Hank said.

"I made it disappear," Nathan told him. "Let's go back to the cabin. I want to play your video game. Can I?" he asked Hank.

"One time," Hank said. "But that's all. You're going to be much too busy!"

Far out in the water a fish jumped. Two

small frogs hopped onto the pier.

"Well, boys," Aunt Paula said, gathering up the poles, "one week from tomorrow your mother's coming to take you home. What do you want to do until then?"

Hank grinned at Nathan.

Nathan wiped his mouth on his sleeve again.

"I think," Hank said, "we'll just go fish."

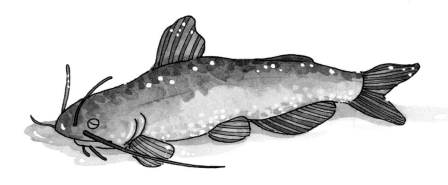